# YES WITH CRACKERS

## THREE FUNNY STORIES

**Nelson Canada**

## ACKNOWLEDGEMENTS

For each of the selections listed below, grateful acknowledgement is made for permission to reprint original or copyrighted material, as follows:

### Blue Moose

by Manus Pinkwater, copyright © 1975 by Manus Pinkwater. Reprinted by permission of G. P. Putnam's Sons.

### The Bungalo Boys III: Champions of Hockey

John Bianchi © Bungalo Books.

### The Boy Who Turned Into a TV Set

by Stephen Manes, drawings by Michael Bass, text copyright © 1979 by Stephen Manes, illustrations copyright © 1979 by Michael Bass. Reprinted by permission of Coward, McCann & Geoghegan.

Houghton Mifflin WAVES: Language Across the Curriculum
PUBLISHED SIMULTANEOUSLY IN 1993 BY:

Nelson Canada,
A Division of Thomson
Canada Limited
1120 Birchmount Road
Scarborough, Ontario
M1K 5G4

Houghton Mifflin Company
222 Berkeley Street
Boston, MA
02116-3764

© Nelson Canada,
A Division of Thomson Canada Limited, 1993

Printed in Canada

### Canadian Cataloguing in Publication Data

Main entry under title:
Yes, with crackers

(Waves: language across the curriculum)
Contents: Blue moose / written and illustrated by Manus Pinkwater—Bungalo boys III: champions of hockey / written and illustrated by John Bianchi—The boy who turned into a tv set / by Stephen Manes; illustrated by Michael Bass.

ISBN 17-604278-4

1. Children's stories, American.   2. Children's stories, Canadian (English).*  3. Humorous stories, American.   4. Humorous stories, Canadian (English).*  I. Pinkwater, Daniel Manus. Blue moose.  II. Bianchi, John. Bungalo boys III.   III. Manes, Stephen. The boy who turned into a tv set.  IV. Series.

PZ5.Y47     1993      j813'.5408      C91-095373-2

1 2 3 4 5 6 / TRI / 9 9 8 7 6 5 4 3

DESIGN AND ART DIRECTION: Pronk&Associates

COLOUR SEPARATIONS AND FILM WORK: Colborne, Cox & Burns Inc.

# CONTENTS

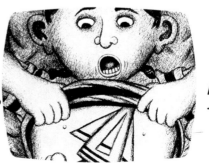

# Blue Moose

**Written and illustrated by Manus Pinkwater**

*The moose shines bright,*
*The stars give a light,*
*And you may kiss a porcupine*
*At ten o'clock at night.*

———————

*The moose is blue,*
*Your wish will come true.*

## Moose Meeting

Mr. Breton had a little restaurant on the edge of the big woods. There was nothing north of Mr. Breton's house except nothing, with trees in between. When winter came, the north wind blew through the trees and froze everything solid. Then it would snow. Mr. Breton didn't like it.

Mr. Breton was a very good cook. Every day, people from the town came to his restaurant. They ate gallons of his special clam chowder. They ate plates of his special beef stew. They ate fish stew and Mr. Breton's special homemade bread. The people from the town never talked much and they never said anything about his cooking.

"Did you like your clam chowder?" Mr. Breton would ask.

"Yup," the people from the town would say.

Mr. Breton wished they would say, "Delicious!" or, "Good chowder, Breton!" All they ever said was, "Yup." In winter they came on skis and snowshoes.

Every morning Mr. Breton went out behind his house to get firewood. He wore three sweaters, a scarf, galoshes, a woolen hat, a big checkered coat, and mittens. He still felt cold. Sometimes animals came out of the woods to watch Mr. Breton. Raccoons and rabbits came. The cold didn't bother them. It bothered Mr. Breton even more when they watched him.

One morning there was a moose in Mr. Breton's yard. It was a blue moose. When Mr. Breton went out his back door, the moose was there, looking at him. After a while, Mr. Breton went back in, closed the door, and made a pot of coffee while he waited for the moose to go away. It didn't go away; it just stood in Mr. Breton's yard, looking at his back door. Mr. Breton drank a cup of coffee. The moose stood in the yard. Mr. Breton opened the door again. "Shoo! Go away!" he said.

It was a blue moose.

"Do you mind if I come in and get warm?" the moose said.
"I'm just about frozen." The moose brushed past him and
walked into the kitchen. His antlers almost touched the ceiling.
The moose sat down on the floor next to Mr. Breton's stove. He
closed his eyes and sat leaning toward the stove for a long time. Mr.
Breton stood in the kitchen, looking at the moose. The moose didn't
move. Wisps of steam began to rise from his blue fur. After a long
time the moose sighed. It sounded like a foghorn.

"Can I get you a cup of coffee?" Mr. Breton asked the moose.
"Or some clam chowder?"

"Clam chowder," said the moose.

Mr. Breton filled a bowl with creamy clam chowder

and set it on the floor. The moose dipped his big nose into the bowl and snuffled up the chowder. He made a sort of slurping, whistling noise.

"Sir," the moose said, "this is wonderful clam chowder."

Mr. Breton blushed a very deep red. "Do you really mean that?"

"Sir," the moose said, "I have eaten some very good chowder in my time, and yours is the very best."

"Oh my," said Mr. Breton, blushing even redder. "Oh my. Would you like some more?"

"Yes, with crackers," said the moose.

The moose ate seventeen bowls of chowder with crackers. Then he had twelve pieces of hot gingerbread and forty-eight cups of coffee. While the moose slurped and whistled, Mr. Breton sat in a chair. Every now and then he said to himself, "Oh my. The

The people from the town were surprised to see the moose.

best he's ever eaten. Oh my."

Later, when some people from the town came to Mr. Breton's house, the moose met them at the door. "How many in your party, please?" the moose asked. "I have a table for you; please follow me."

The people from the town were surprised to see the moose. They felt like running away, but they were too surprised. The moose led them to a table, brought them menus, looked at each person, snorted, and clumped into the kitchen.

"There are some people outside; I'll take care of them," he told Mr. Breton.

The people were whispering to one another about the moose, when he clumped back to the table.

"Are you ready to order?"

"Yup," the people from the town said. They waited for the moose to ask them if they would like some chowder, the way Mr. Breton always did. But the moose just stared at them as though they were very foolish. The people felt uncomfortable. "We'll have the clam chowder."

"Chaudière de Clam; very good," the moose said. "Do you desire crackers or homemade bread?"

"We will have crackers," said the people from the town.

"I suggest you have the bread; it is hot," said the moose.

"We will have bread," said the people from the town.

"And for dessert," said the moose, "will you have fresh gingerbread or Apple Jacquette?"

"What do you recommend?" asked the people from the town.

"After the Chaudière de Clam, the gingerbread is best."

"Thank you," said the people from the town.

But the moose just stared at them as though they were very foolish.

"It is my pleasure to serve you," said the moose. The moose brought bowls of chowder balanced on his antlers.

At the end of the meal, the moose clumped to the table. "Has everything been to your satisfaction?" he asked.

"Yup," said the people from the town, their mouths full of gingerbread.

"I beg your pardon?" said the moose. "What did you say?"

"It was very good," said the people from the town. "It was the best we've ever eaten."

"I will tell the chef," said the moose.

The moose clumped into the kitchen and told Mr. Breton that the people from the town had said that the food was the best they had ever eaten. Mr. Breton rushed out of the kitchen and out of the house. The people from the town were sitting on the porch, putting on their snowshoes.

"Did you tell the moose that my clam chowder was the best you've ever eaten?" Mr. Breton asked.

"Yup," said the people from the town, "we said that. We think that you are the best

cook in the world; we have always thought so."

"Always?" asked Mr. Breton.

"Of course," the people from the town said. "Why do you think we walk seven miles on snowshoes just to eat here?"

The people from the town walked away on their snowshoes. Mr. Breton sat on the edge of the porch and thought it over. When the moose came out to see why Mr. Breton was sitting outside without his coat on, Mr. Breton said, "Do you know, those people think I am the best cook in the whole world?"

"Of course they do," the moose said. "Do you want me to go into town to get some crackers? We seem to have run out."

"Yes," said Mr. Breton, "and get some asparagus too. I'm going to cook something special tomorrow."

"By the way," said the moose, "aren't you cold out here?"

"No, I'm not the least bit cold," Mr. Breton said. "This is turning out to be a very mild winter."

## Game Warden

There was a lot of talk in town about the moose at Mr. Breton's restaurant. Some people who had never been there before went to the restaurant just to see the moose. There was an article in the newspaper about the moose, and how he talked to the customers, and brought them their bowls of clam chowder, and helped Mr. Breton in the kitchen.

Some people from other towns drove a long way with chains on their tires to Mr. Breton's restaurant, just to see the moose. Mr. Breton was always very busy waiting on tables at lunchtime and suppertime.

The moose was always very polite to the people, but he made them feel a little uncomfortable too. He looked at people with only one eye at a time, and he was better than most of them at pronouncing French words. He knew what kind of wine to drink with clam chowder, and he knew which kind of wine to drink with the special beef stew. Some of the people in the town bragged that the moose was a friend of theirs, and always gave them a table right away. When they came to the restaurant they would pat the moose on the back, and say, "Hello, Moose, you remember me, don't you?"

"There will be a slight delay until a table is ready," the moose would say, and snort, and shake himself.

Mr. Breton was very happy in the kitchen. There were pots of all sorts of good things steaming on the stove and smelling good, and bread baking in the oven from morning to night. Mr. Breton loved to cook good things for lots of people, the more the better. He had never been so busy and happy in his life.

One morning, Mr. Bobowicz, the game warden, came to the restaurant. "Mr. Breton, are you aware of Section 5—Subheading 6—Paragraph 3 of the state fish and game laws?" said Mr. Bobowicz.

"No, I am not aware of Section 5—Subheading 6— Paragraph 3," Mr. Breton said.

"In short, it is against the law to have a tame moose."

"What is it all about?"

"No person shall keep a moose as a pet, tie up a moose, keep a moose in a pen or barn, or parlor or bedroom, or any such enclosure," said Mr. Bobowicz. "In short, it is against the law to have a tame moose."

"Oh my," said Mr. Breton, "I don't want to do anything against the law. But I don't keep the moose. He just came along one day, and has stayed ever since. He helps me run my restaurant."

The moose just fit in the bed, if he folded up his feet.

Mr. Bobowicz rubbed his chin. "And where is the aforesaid moose?"

Mr. Breton had given the moose one of the rooms upstairs, in which there was a particularly large bed. The moose just fit in the bed, if he folded up his feet. He liked it very much; he said he never had a bed of his own. The moose slept on the bed under six blankets, and during the day he would go upstairs sometimes, and stretch out on the bed and sigh with pleasure.

When Mr. Bobowicz came to see Mr. Breton, the moose had been downstairs to help Mr. Breton eat a giant breakfast, and then he had wandered back to his room to enjoy lying on his bed until the lunchtime customers arrived. He heard Mr. Breton and Mr. Bobowicz talking. The moose bugled. He had never bugled in Mr. Breton's house before. Bugling is a noise that no animal except a moose can really do right. Elk can bugle, and elephants can bugle, and some kinds of geese and swans can bugle, but it is nothing like moose bugling. When the moose bugled, the whole house jumped and rattled, dishes clinked together in the cupboard, pots and pans clanged together, icicles fell off the house.

"I AM NOT A TAME MOOSE!" the moose shouted from where he was lying on his bed.

Mr. Bobowicz looked at Mr. Breton with very wide eyes. "Was that the moose?"

The moose had gotten out of bed, and was clumping down the stairs. "You're flipping right, that was the moose," he growled.

The moose clumped right up to Mr. Bobowicz, and looked at him with one red eye. The moose's nose was touching Mr. Bobowicz's nose. They just stood there, looking

The moose's nose was touching

Mr. Bobowicz's nose.

23

at each other, for a long time. The moose was breathing loudly, and his eye seemed to be a glowing coal. Mr. Bobowicz's knees were shaking. Then the moose spoke very slowly. "You . . . are . . . a . . . tame . . . game warden."

The moose turned, and clumped back up the stairs. Mr. Breton and Mr. Bobowicz heard him sigh and heard the springs crash and groan as he flopped onto the big bed.

"Mr. Bobowicz, the moose is not tame," Mr. Breton said. "He is a wild moose, and he lives here of his own free will; he is the headwaiter." Mr. Breton spoke very quietly, because Mr. Bobowicz had not moved since the moose had come downstairs. His eyes were still open very wide, and his knees were still shaking. Mr. Breton took Mr. Bobowicz by the hand, and led him into the kitchen and poured him a cup of coffee.

## Dave

Not very far from Mr. Breton's house, in a secret place in the woods, lived a hermit named Dave. Everybody knew that Dave was out there, but nobody ever saw him. Mr. Bobowicz, the game warden, had seen what might have been Dave a couple of times; or it might have been a shadow. Sometimes, late at night, Mr. Breton would hear the wind whistling strangely, and think of Dave.

The moose brought Dave home with him one night. They were old friends. Dave was dressed in rabbit skins, stitched together. His feet were wrapped in tree bark and moose-moss. An owl sat on his head.

...Dave played on the whistle,

like the wind making strange sounds....

"Dave is very shy," the moose said. "He would appreciate it if you didn't say anything to him until he knows you better, maybe in ten or fifteen years. He knows about your gingerbread, and he would like to try it." While the moose spoke, Dave blushed very red, and tried to cover his face with the owl, which fluttered and squawked.

Mr. Breton put dishes with gingerbread and applesauce and fresh whipped cream in front of Dave, the moose, and the owl. There was no noise but the moose slurping, and Dave's spoon scraping. Mr. Breton turned to get the coffeepot. When he looked back at the table, Dave and the owl were gone.

"Dave says thank you," the moose said.

The next night Dave was back, and this time he had a whistle made out of a turkey bone in his hat. After the gingerbread, Dave played on the whistle, like the wind making strange sounds, the moose hummed, and Mr. Breton clicked two spoons, while the owl hopped up and down on the kitchen table, far into the night.

**Hums of a Moose**

One day, after the moose had been staying with Mr. Breton for a fairly long time, there was an especially heavy snowfall. The snow got to be as high as the house, and there was no way for people to come from the town.

Mr. Breton got a big fire going in the stove, and kept adding pieces of wood until the stove was glowing red. The house was warm, and filled with the smell of applesauce, which Mr. Breton was cooking in big pots on the stove. Mr. Breton was peeling apples and the moose was sitting on the floor, lapping every now and then at a big chowder bowl full of coffee on the kitchen table.

The kitchen floor had turned into a meadow....

The moose didn't say anything. Mr. Breton didn't say anything. Now and then the moose would take a deep breath with his nose in the air, sniffing in the smell of apples and cinnamon and raisins cooking. Then he would sigh. The sighs got louder and longer.

The moose began to hum—softly, then louder. The humming made the table shake, and Mr. Breton felt the humming in his fingers each time he picked up an apple. The humming mixed with the apple and cinnamon smell and melted the frost on the windows, and the room filled with sunlight. Mr. Breton smelled flowers.

Then he could see them. The kitchen floor had turned into a meadow with new grass, dandelions, periwinkles, and daisies.

The moose hummed. Mr. Breton smelled melting snow. He heard ice cracking. He felt the ground shake under the hoofs of moose returning from the low, wet places. Rabbits bounded through the fields. Bears, thin after the winter's sleep, came out of hiding. Birds sang.

The people in the town could not remember such an unseasonable thaw. The weather got warm all of a sudden, and the ice and snow melted for four days before winter set in again. When they went to Mr. Breton's restaurant, they discovered that he had made a wonderful stew with lots of carrots that reminded them of meadows in springtime.

## Moose Moving

When spring finally came, the moose became moody. He spent a lot of time staring out the back door. Flocks of geese flew overhead, returning to lakes in the North, and the moose always stirred when he heard their honking.

"Chef," the moose said one morning, "I will be going tomorrow. I wonder if you would pack some gingerbread for me to take along."

Mr. Breton baked a special batch of gingerbread, and packed it in parcels tied with string, so the moose could hang them from his antlers. When the moose came downstairs, Mr. Breton was sitting in the kitchen drinking coffee. The parcels of gingerbread were on the kitchen table.

"Do you want a bowl of coffee before you go?" Mr. Breton asked.

"Thank you," said the moose.

"I shall certainly miss you," Mr. Breton said.

"Thank you," said the moose.

"You are the best friend I have," said Mr. Breton.

"Thank you," said the moose.

"Do you suppose you'll ever come back?" Mr. Breton asked.

"Not before Thursday or Friday," said the moose. "It would be impolite to visit my uncle for less than a week."

The moose hooked his antlers into the loops of string on the packages of gingerbread. "My uncle will like this." He stood up and turned to the door.

"Have a nice time at your uncle's," said Mr. Breton.

"Wait!" Mr. Breton shouted. "Do you mean that you are not leaving forever? I thought you were lonely for the life of a wild moose. I thought you wanted to go back to the wild, free places."

"Chef, do you have any idea of how cold it gets in the wild, free places?" the moose said. "And the food! Terrible! "

"Have a nice time at your uncle's," said Mr. Breton.

"I'll send you a postcard," said the moose.

# The Bungalo Boys III

By John Bianchi

## Champions of HOCKEY

**Written and illustrated by John Bianchi**

The swoosh of steel on ice. The clatter of stick and puck. Sounds that crackle through frosted morning air. Sounds of the Bungalo Boys preparing for competition—a contest of skill, strength, grace and pluck. Sounds of hockey—the world's fastest game!

At stake is the symbol of hockey supremacy—the Bungalo Birdbath, installed by Great-Great-Granduncle Guido de Bungalo in 1889. Family tradition plays a big part in all Birdbath games. For 99 years, the Bath has been successfully defended against all challengers by the Bungalo sports dynasty. Indeed, many feel that the ghosts of these great hockey legends haunt the beaver pond to this very day.

At stake is the symbol of hockey supremacy....

This year's challengers are a mystery team from the Natural Hockey League. As player-coach Ma Bungalo puts her boys through their pregame skate, anxious eyes search the visitors' end of the ice. Finally, three small figures appear.

"It's a bunch of penguins!" laughs Curly. The rest of the boys cannot resist a moment of mirth. But their laughter is short-lived. Out of the morning haze, like three great ocean tankers clearing a fog, lumbers the rest of the NHL's team . . .

## . . . the Bruins.

The icy determination that once flowed through the boys' veins quickly turns to Zamboni slush.

Ma Bungalo rallies her boys. She and Rufus will play defence with Projectile "The Wonder Dog" in goal. Johnny-Bob will play right wing, with Curly "The Cannon" on the left side. Ma encourages Shorty to play centre.

Ma encourages Shorty to play centre.

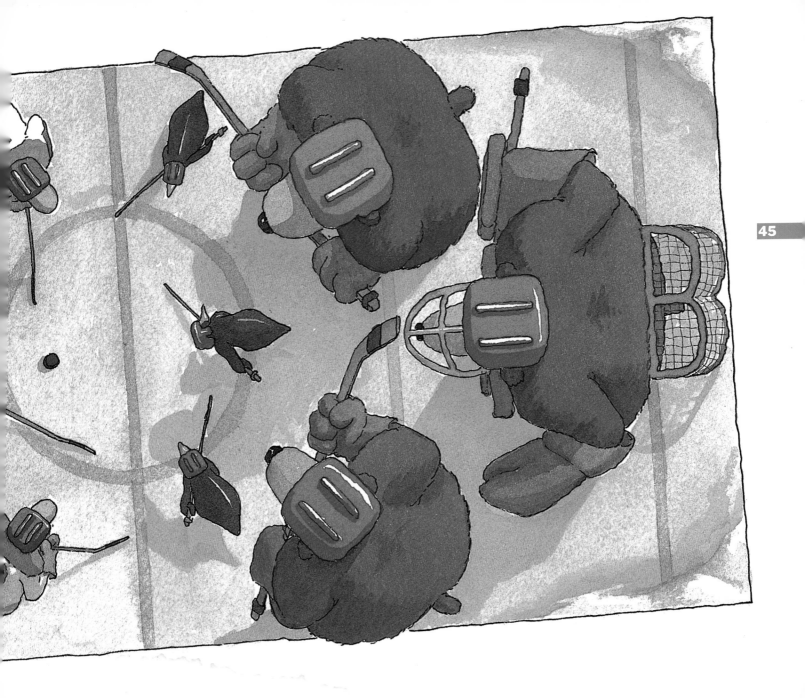

The NHL counters with its famous "Bird" line. The Bruins will play defence. All agree to use the honour system and call their own penalties.

The boys get off to a slow start. Little Shorty plays giveaway in his own end, and one of the big Bruin defencebears easily converts the miscue. NHL: one. Bungalos: no score.

Then, after going down to block a shot, Little Shorty coughs up the puck. Projectile is helpless as one of the Penguins wastes no time turning on the red light. NHL: two. Bungalos: no score.

Midway through the second period, Little Shorty takes a costly penalty and quickly sends himself to the penalty box. Inspired by the loss of their little centre, the Bungalos capitalize on their one-man disadvantage and score two unanswered goals. NHL: two. Bungalos: two.

In the third period, the NHL launches an all-out attack. The team pulls its big bruin goalie and fore-checks the Bungalos into their own end. The beaver pond has never seen such heavy action!

Suddenly, with a sickening "**CA-SPLASH**," the ice shatters!

Out of the mayhem drifts a lone skater with the puck. Little Shorty has a breakaway!

With time running out on the clock and his brothers offering words of encouragement, Little Shorty stickhandles toward the NHL's empty net. Some fans start a wave. The organist plays. Guided by the legendary Bungalo ghosts, Little Shorty takes careful aim. He shoots…

DON'T MISS SLUSH HEAD!

During the post-game celebrations, the Bungalo Boys congratulate each other on a game well played.

"We're still number one!" roars Curly.

"We never gave up!" shouts Johnny-Bob.

"We just did what we had to do!" cries Rufus.

"It was 60 minutes of teamwork," notes Ma.

**"Cause we're the Champions of Hockey!"** they all scream.

"And best of all," adds Little Shorty with relief, "no one got into a fight."

...the Bungalo Boys congratulate each other on a game well played.

# THE BOY WHO TURNED INTO A TV SET

Written by Stephen Manes
Illustrated by Michael Bass

**ONE**

59

Ogden Pettibone watched television all the time. He watched game shows and news shows, police shows and educational shows, comedies and dramas, public service announcements, weather reports, cartoons, and commercials. Ogden would watch anything. Except soap operas. Ogden thought soap operas were dumb.

"If you keep watching TV so much," his mother often told him, "you might just turn into a television." Ogden always laughed when she said that. He knew she was only kidding. He knew people didn't really turn into TV sets.

One horrible day after school, Ogden came home to find that the Pettibones' television was broken.

"Broken!" he screamed. "How could it be broken?"

"It doesn't get a picture, and the only sound it makes is a sizzling noise, and smoke comes from the back when you turn it on," said his mother. "Someone will come out and fix it tomorrow."

"Tomorrow!" Ogden wailed. "But I need to watch my programs today!"

"Read a book for a change," Mrs. Pettibone suggested.

"Phooey," said Ogden, but he took his mother's advice. He went to the bookshelf and looked for a volume called *How to Repair Your Own TV*. Skimming through it, he found the information he was looking for. "No picture; sizzling, smoke: BIG TROUBLE. Do not attempt to fix this yourself, or you will be sorry. Unplug the set and call a repairman."

Ogden frowned, put the book back on the shelf, had some milk and cake, and watched his goldfish swim around the aquarium. It was slightly more interesting than staring at the blank TV screen.

"Dinnertime!" his father finally shouted from the kitchen.

Ogden opened his mouth to say he'd be right there, but instead a deep voice came out. "We'll be right back after this important message," it said. Ogden was very surprised.

"Don't be funny, Ogden," his dad scolded.

"I've never seen clothes so white!" Ogden exclaimed in a woman's voice that startled him even more. "How do you do it?"

His mother frowned. "Og, what's wrong with you? Come to dinner while it's hot."

Ogden sat down at the table. "I use Ultra Wash," he said in another woman's voice. "It has twenty-seven percent more cleaning power." This wasn't what Ogden wanted to say at all. It was just what came out of his mouth when he opened it and tried to speak. He couldn't understand it.

"Enough, Ogden," said his father. "I don't think you're amusing."

Neither did Ogden. He felt as though he were a dummy on the lap of some invisible ventriloquist. "Ultra Wash gets your clothes so bright, your friends will not believe the sight!" a chorus sang cheerfully through his lips. Embarrassed, Ogden slumped down in his chair.

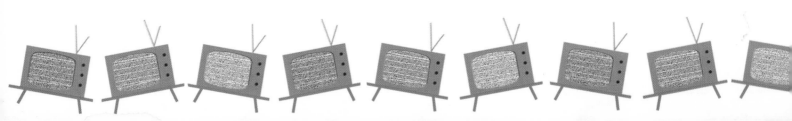

"Sit up straight and stop this foolishness," his mother commanded. "If you can't behave, you'll go up to your room without supper. Now, tell us what you did in school today."

Ogden thought he must be going crazy. He tried to tell them about the guinea pig that had triplets, but what came out of his mouth was someone else's voice saying, "Well, that just about wraps up our show."

"It certainly does!" snapped his mother. "Go up to your room, and don't come back till you're ready to behave."

Ogden wanted to protest. But when he opened his mouth, a voice said, "See you same time tomorrow."

"Get going! Right now!" his father shouted.

Ogden left the table. He plodded up the stairs and flopped down on his bed. "I can't understand it!" he said to himself, making very sure he didn't open his mouth. "What's happening to me?"

He let out a big sigh. Before he had a chance to finish it, a new voice squealed with glee. "Whee!" it exclaimed. "I've been chocolatized!"

Ogden clapped his hand over his mouth to keep anything else from coming out. Whatever was going on, it was worse than a bad case of hiccups.

In fact, it was a lot like hiccups. Ogden tried holding his breath. But after a while he began turning blue and had to come up for air. "Good evening," a robust voice said as Ogden gasped. "President Ablefinger announced today that he believes more money should be spent on peanut butter research."

Ogden slammed his jaws shut. Maybe some water would help. He went to the bathroom and filled a cup. But as he opened his mouth to take a sip, he heard an elderly voice say, "False teeth a problem?" The water drowned the next words out, but when the glass was empty, the voice declared, "I can eat anything now!" and took a loud chomp on an invisible apple.

Hiccup cures didn't always work on Ogden's hiccups, and it was obvious they weren't going to work on this problem, either. He went into his bedroom, turned out the lights, lay down on his bed, closed his eyes, and tried to think.

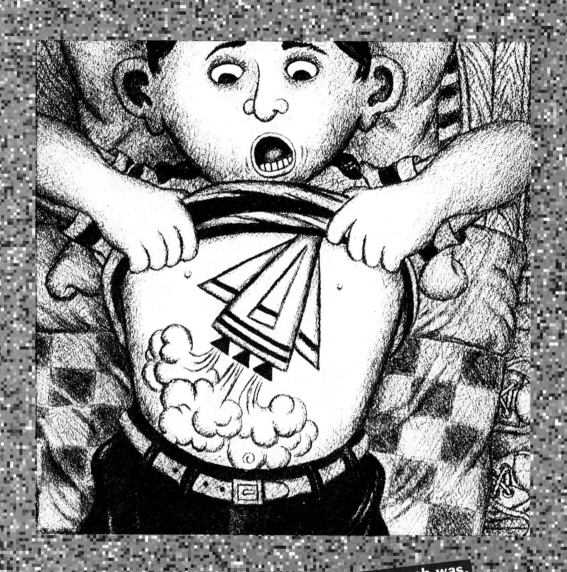

The T-shirt wasn't glowing at all. His stomach was.

It wasn't much use. He didn't have any idea what was the matter with him. And how could he explain his predicament to his parents if every time he opened his mouth, something stupid came out? He sighed again. "A swarm of giant fruit flies attacked the town of Quagmire, Montana, today," said his lips in a resonant baritone.

Ogden shut his mouth and opened his eyes. Suddenly he noticed that his T-shirt seemed to be glowing. He untucked it to take a closer look.

The T-shirt wasn't glowing at all. His stomach was. Right above his bellybutton was the six o'clock news in living color. A rocket on his tummy-screen blasted off toward his chest.

Ogden's jaw dropped in amazement, and he bellowed a deafening rocketlike roar. "Wow!" he thought, "I've turned into a TV!"

# TWO

Ogden's parents heard the blastoff.

"What's all that racket? Are you okay?" his father hollered, rushing up the stairs.

Ogden kept his mouth shut.

"Did you fall out of bed or something? What was all that noise?"

Ogden pointed to his belly. The rocket disappeared into the clouds.

"It's the six o'clock news!" his father cried. "But where's the sound?"

Ogden pointed to his mouth and opened wide. "Tomorrow the astronauts will attempt the first game of baseball ever played in outer space," he said in the voice of the reporter who appeared on the screen. Then he closed his mouth again.

"Open up a minute," his father said, "I want to hear whether they caught those sneak thieves."

Ogden obediently loosened his jaws. The criminals were still at large, but the police had recovered the stolen truckload of tennis shoes.

"What's going on here?" Mrs. Pettibone wanted to know.

"Ogden's turned into a TV set," his father explained.

"I always said he would," his mother gloated.

"How did it happen?" his father asked him.

Ogden shrugged. He knew as little about it as they did.

"Well, enough's enough," said his mother. "Shut yourself off and come back down to dinner."

Ogden shook his head.

"Why not?" His father scowled.

Ogden grabbed a pad and pencil from his desk and scribbled the words, "I can't."

"Don't be ridiculous," his father said.

Ogden scribbled furiously. "I'm telling the truth," he wrote. "I don't know how this happened. I can't shut myself off. And I can't talk, because every time I open my mouth, TV sounds come out."

"Hmmmm," his father hummed thoughtfully.

"What shall we do?" his mother worried.

"I think we'd better have the doctor take a look at Ogden in the morning."

"And in the meantime?" Ogden wrote.

"Well, as long as our TV's broken, you might as well make yourself useful," his father replied. "Come downstairs and let us watch you."

Ogden ate supper. He felt rather uncomfortable making TV sounds between each bite, but his parents were very understanding.

Then they all went into the living room. Ogden sat in front of the broken television and took off his T-shirt. While his parents stared at him from the couch, he watched his amazing belly in a mirror at their feet. The mirror made the picture look backward, but he preferred that to the topsy-turvy view and stiff neck he got when he looked straight down at his screen.

"Excellent reception," said his father during a commercial break, "even though the picture is a bit small. And this remote control is the best yet. If we want the sound louder, all we have to do is ask. Maybe we won't have to have our old set fixed after all."

"But Ogden only gets one channel," Mrs. Pettibone reminded her husband.

Ogden sat in front of the broken television and took off his T-shirt.

"Forgot about that," said Mr. Pettibone.

Ogden hoped they weren't serious. Much as he enjoyed being the center of attention, he still felt funny about his glowing stomach and contrary vocal cords. He hoped the doctor would be able to figure out what was wrong with him.

"Open up, dear," Mrs. Pettibone requested. "The commercial's over."

Ogden sighed into action.

## THREE

The new television did not sleep well that night. The glow from his screen didn't shine through the covers, but his mouth occasionally fell open as he dozed off, and then a loud commercial or an audience howling at a comedian's joke would waken him.

He was tired and hungry when he came down to breakfast, but his parents asked him not to eat until the commercials came on so that they wouldn't miss any of the morning news. Ogden obliged them, but he did feel rather chilly sitting at the table without a shirt on.

After breakfast, he and his father rode to the doctor's office on a bus. It was crowded, but they found two seats together, and everything was fine until Ogden yawned.

"I hate to be the one to tell you this," a girl's voice said through his mouth, "but you have bad breath."

"WHAT?" stormed the enormous woman beside him. "Who said that?"

"Bad breath," the voice repeated before Ogden could close his jaws.

"I do *not*!" the woman huffed. "I don't know who you think you are, but you had better apologize, sonny!"

Ogden would have liked to, but he knew there was no telling what might come out if he opened his mouth again. He kept it shut.

"Please excuse him," his father told the woman. "I'm sure he didn't mean it."

"Then why did he say it? The least he can do is apologize for himself."

"He really is sorry," said Mr. Pettibone. "Aren't you, Ogden?"

Ogden nodded.

"You didn't mean it, did you?"

Ogden shook his head.

"Humph," the woman sniffed, and turned away.

"Who said that?"

Just then the bus went over a bump in the road, jolting its passengers so violently that Ogden's jaw dropped open again. "Do you have trouble losing weight?" asked an announcer's voice before Ogden could get himself under control.

The huge woman turned bright red and looked as though she might explode any second. Mr. Pettibone whisked his son to the exit, and marched him off the bus.

"I know it wasn't your fault," Mr. Pettibone told Ogden as they walked toward the doctor's office, "but please try to keep your mouth closed. We wouldn't want another unpleasant incident."

Ogden nodded and clenched his teeth.

The doctor's waiting room was filled with sick kids and their parents. Ogden found a book on airplanes and sat down beside his father to read it.

"My name's Jennifer," said a runny-nosed little girl who came up to him. "What's yours?"

Ogden didn't want to be unfriendly, but he thought he'd better not try to say anything.

"Hey! I said what's your name!"

Ogden just smiled, keeping his lips tight.

"Tell me your name!" the girl insisted, jumping in the air and landing right on Ogden's toes.

Ogden opened his mouth to say "Ow!" but what came out instead was a lionlike roar: "GRRRRRRRRRR!" It sounded so realistic, it scared little Jennifer back to her mother.

"Quite a cough your son has," commented the woman sitting next to Ogden's father. "I certainly hope it isn't contagious." Mr. Pettibone shook his head.

The nurse led Ogden and his father to an examining room. "The doctor will be with you shortly," she told Ogden. "Please take off all your clothes except your underpants."

Ogden did. He checked his screen. It was showing a soap opera, so he didn't bother to open his mouth to listen.

"Hello, Ogden," Doctor Stark said cheerfully when he came in a few minutes later. "What seems to be the trouble?"

Ogden pointed to the picture on his stomach. His father explained the problem.

"Hmmmm," said the doctor, bending over to take a look. "Unusual." He pointed a tongue depressor toward Ogden's mouth. "Say 'ah.' "

Ogden tried. What came out instead was a woman's voice saying, "I'm afraid there's not much hope for Penny after that terrible auto accident."

"Hmmmm," said the doctor again, and peered intently at Ogden's screen.

"Do you think it's serious?" his father asked.

"Oh, Penny will pull through," Doctor Stark reassured him. "She has to. She's the star of the show."

"But what about Ogden?" Mr. Pettibone wondered.

"Hmmmm," said Doctor Stark. He put his stethoscope in his ears and listened to his patient's chest, stomach, back, and neck. He examined Ogden's eyes and ears. Then he stuck a thermometer in Ogden's mouth and watched the soap opera for three minutes, even though he couldn't hear what the actors were saying, since Ogden had to keep his mouth closed. Finally Doctor Stark took the thermometer out again.

"No fever," he said. "Ogden, I'm afraid there's nothing I can do for you."

"But he can't even speak for himself," Mr. Pettibone protested. "Is it something like laryngitis?"

"It's a much more difficult case than that, I'm afraid. Ogden has televisionosis."

"Televisionosis?" Ogden wanted to ask. Mr. Pettibone asked it for him.

"Yes," Doctor Stark replied. "It's a disease so rare it's practically unheard of. I've certainly never heard of it before. One of my patients used to get radio stations on his tooth fillings, but this is much more severe. Your boy is exhibiting all the symptoms of a television set."

"But he doesn't want to be a television set."

"I'm afraid he has no choice. There's no known cure for televisionosis."

"Oh, my," said Mr. Pettibone, too stunned to say anything else.

"Perhaps he'll outgrow it," said the doctor pleasantly. "And if he doesn't, he'll be very popular. Everybody loves television."

## FOUR

Ogden felt miserable. He didn't want to be a television the rest of his life, no matter how popular he might be. He decided he would pretend he was not a television, and he went to school that afternoon as if everything were normal.

But when his math teacher asked him what eleven times twelve was, Ogden told her in a very authoritative voice that she had smelly feet. She sent him to the principal's office.

When the principal asked him how he felt about what he'd done, Ogden whispered that she had perspiration odor. She made him stay late after school.

And when he got home and met his friends, Ogden told them matter-of-factly that they had ugly pimples. They refused to play with him. They wouldn't even look his way when he tried to show them his TV screen. Ogden whimpered like the hungry puppy who appeared on his belly, and sadly went home.

The TV repairwoman, Mrs. Turkel, was in the living room working on the broken set. Ogden watched her take it apart and replace some burnt-out tubes. Then she put it back together again. It worked beautifully.

Ogden suddenly had an idea. "Can you fix me, too?" he wrote on a scrap of paper. He handed it to the repairwoman and pulled up his T-shirt.

"Don't be silly, Ogden," Mrs. Pettibone scolded.

She poked his nose.

The repairwoman stared at Ogden's screen. "Perhaps there *is* something I can do," she said. "Open wide."

Ogden did. "And for a limited time only…"

"Close, please," Mrs. Turkel interrupted. Ogden obeyed.

"Your picture's perfect, and so's your sound," she told him. "What's the problem?"

"He doesn't want to be a television," Mrs. Pettibone explained.

"You don't?" exclaimed the repairwoman, shaking a finger at Ogden. "Why in the world not? Televisions are the greatest invention in the history of civilization. What other invention lets you watch old movies, bowling tournaments, and congressional hearings in the comfort of your own home while you eat a tuna fish sandwich? No other invention, that's what! You don't want to be a television? Try being a garbage disposer and see how you like that!"

Ogden could hardly say anything to disagree.

"At least he'd like to be able to change channels once in a while," said Mrs. Pettibone.

"Well, why didn't you say so?" said the repairwoman, taking a screwdriver from behind her ear. "Where's his channel selector?"

"That's just it," Mrs. Pettibone said. "I don't think he has one."

"Nonsense! Every television has one. You just have to know where it is."

Mrs. Turkel took her screwdriver and tapped it gently on Ogden's head. Nothing happened. She tapped his forehead. Still nothing happened. She poked his nose. Suddenly, the commercial on Ogden's screen disappeared, and a game show took its place. "Open wide, please," said the repairwoman. Ogden did.

"True or false? Every three-toed sloth actually has six toenails," the quizmaster asked. The repairwoman poked Ogden's nose again.

The quizmaster disappeared, and a picture of a small living room took his place. "Ay-yi-yi!" hollered a funny-looking man who ran into the room and tore his hair. "How could a rhinoceros run into our car when it was in the garage all day?" An unseen audience screamed with laughter.

"Close, please," said Mrs. Turkel. Ogden did. He felt a little better. He still didn't like being a TV, but at least now he had a choice of programs.

"Well, that problem's solved," said Mrs. Turkel. "Anything else?"

"It would be nice if he could turn himself off some of the time," said Mrs. Pettibone. Ogden nodded agreement.

"Just use his switch," said Mrs. Turkel.

"But where is it?" Ogden's mother asked.

"Right here, of course," said the repairwoman, and she poked her screwdriver gently into Ogden's bellybutton. His picture suddenly disappeared, and his stomach looked exactly the way it used to, except for a little white dot in the middle. And that quickly faded, too.

By now Ogden was accustomed to keeping his mouth shut, since opening it usually seemed to get him into trouble, so it took him a little while to think of trying his voice again. "Does this mean I can talk?" he finally asked. His ears gave him the answer.

"Hooray!" he shouted. "I'm not a TV anymore!"

"Of course you are," said Mrs. Turkel. "Poke your bellybutton and see for yourself."

Ogden did. His stomach lit up again, and his mouth said, "Never before and never again will this offer…" He poked his navel once more. The picture and sound cut off instantly.

"You see?" cried the repairwoman triumphantly. "You're as good a television as any I've ever fixed. Now how do you feel about it?"

Ogden wasn't a hundred percent sure. "Better, I guess. It sure is nice to have an off switch."

"Absolutely!" exclaimed the repairwoman. "Anyone who knows anything about televisions will tell you. That's the most important part!"

Ogden couldn't agree more.

## FIVE

Now that he could turn himself on and off, Ogden rather enjoyed being a television, and he watched himself every chance he got. When he did something wrong, his parents couldn't punish him by making him miss his favorite programs. There were no more arguments when Ogden wanted to watch a documentary and his parents wanted to watch cartoons. And as Doctor Stark had predicted, Ogden soon became the most popular kid in his school. Everybody wanted to watch him, and he was delighted to have so many admirers.

His fame spread. TV reporters interviewed him. Newspapers wrote articles about him. And he appeared on the quiz show *Guess What I've Got*, along with a woman who had grown a radish shaped exactly like a dinosaur and a man who owned the world's largest chocolate-covered fish. Unlike the others, Ogden and his TV screen completely stumped the panel, and he won a lifetime supply of marshmallow chickens.

The owner of a department store spotted Ogden on the show and hired him to stand in a window after school and Saturdays alongside the sets the store had for sale. Ogden politely waved at the people who came to stare at him, and he was pleased when they noticed that his picture was by far the sharpest.

But soon he grew tired of being a television. The job in the window began to bore him. His new friends insisted on watching him on the way to school, and when the weather turned cold, he got goose bumps from having nothing on his tummy but a picture. The kids always argued about which programs they should watch, so Ogden's nose soon turned a deep red from their repeated pokings.

Soon Ogden was so sick of being a television, he wouldn't even *watch* TV. He wouldn't sit in the room while his parents watched. He wouldn't even glance at his favorite programs. Finally, he turned himself off and put a piece of tape over his navel so that no one could turn him on.

His fame spread. TV reporters interviewed him.

The store owner was sorry to lose his best attraction. The disappointed kids called their former friend "Ogden the Oddball" and "Obnoxious Ogden" and "Telly-Belly." Mr. and Mrs. Pettibone were concerned. They knew something was wrong with their son, but they didn't know exactly what.

On Thanksgiving Day, Ogden stayed in his room and read a book about monsters instead of watching the annual parades. But late that afternoon, his father shouted from the living room, "Ogden! Come here! Quickly!"

It sounded like an emergency, so Ogden hurried as fast as he could. When he got downstairs, he saw smoke coming from the back of the television set as his father unplugged it.

"Our TV just broke again! The football game's tied with seconds to play!" Mr. Pettibone shouted. "Turn yourself on! Hurry!"

Ogden knew how much football meant to his father. He pulled up his sweater, ripped off the adhesive tape, and poked himself in the bellybutton.

Nothing happened.

"Maybe you didn't press hard enough," his father said, and gave Ogden's navel a healthy poke. Ogden grunted, but nothing appeared on his tummy.

"I don't know what's wrong!" Ogden cried, poking his midriff frantically. "I worked the last time I tried."

"Never mind," said his father. "The game's probably over anyhow. We'll have Mrs. Turkel fix the TV in the morning. Maybe she can fix you, too."

"Not me!" Ogden shouted. "I'm tired of being a TV."

"There's just no pleasing some people," said his mother, shaking her head.

Ogden couldn't believe his nightmare was over. Every few minutes he would poke his bellybutton to make sure, and each time he was delighted when absolutely nothing happened. But now that it was over, he didn't really regret having been a TV. After all, how else would he ever have won a lifetime supply of marshmallow chickens?

At dinner, Ogden silently gave thanks that he wasn't a television anymore. Then he had five helpings of turkey.

"My word, Ogden!" cried his mother when he asked for a sixth. "If you keep eating turkey, you might just turn into a turkey!"

Ogden laughed. He knew she was only kidding. He knew people didn't really turn into turkeys.

But just to be on the safe side, he passed up another helping and saved room for dessert.

THE END